THAT'S GOOD!
THAT'S BAD!
ON SANTA'S JOURNEY

written by
Margery Cuyler

illustrated by
Michael Garland

Henry Holt and Company
New York

Henry Holt and Company, LLC
Publishers since 1866
175 Fifth Avenue
New York, New York 10010
www.HenryHoltKids.com

Library of Congress Cataloging-in-Publication Data
Cuyler, Margery.
That's good! that's bad! on Santa's journey / Margery Cuyler ; illustrated by Michael Garland.—1st ed.
p.   cm.
Summary: While delivering presents on Christmas Eve, accident-prone Santa has a series of mishaps, with both good and bad results.
ISBN-13: 978-0-8050-8777-2 / ISBN-10: 0-8050-8777-X
1. Santa Claus—Juvenile fiction. [1. Santa Claus—Fiction. 2. Christmas—Fiction. 3. Accidents—Fiction.]
I. Garland, Michael, ill. II. Title. III. Title: That is good! that is bad! on Santa's journey.
PZ7.C997Tk 2009   [E]—dc22   2008036816

First Edition—2009
The artist created the illustrations for this book digitally.
Printed in March 2009 in the United States of America by Phoenix Color Corp. d/b/a Lehigh Phoenix, Rockaway, New Jersey, on acid-free paper. ∞

1 3 5 7 9 10 8 6 4 2

For whimsical Tim
—M. C.

For my wife, Peggy
—M. G.

It was Christmas Eve. Santa climbed into his sleigh, kissed Mrs. Claus good-bye, SMOOCH, and told his reindeer to take off, GIDDDYAP!

Oh, that's good.
No, that's bad!

The wind blew, *WHOOSH!* and it began to snow. It snowed so hard that Santa had to land next to an igloo, BRRRR. He thought he'd never get to deliver his presents that night, WHAT A DISASTER!

Oh, that's bad.
No, that's good!

Santa waited for the snow to stop, TICK-TOCK, TICK-TOCK, and finally it did. After leaving some presents at the igloo, he and his reindeer took off again, *WHEEEE!*

Oh, that's good.
No, that's bad!

When Santa reached a little boy's house, the roof was so icy that his reindeer slid across it, SLIPPITY-SLOP, and slammed into the chimney, *CRASH.*

Oh, that's bad.
No, that's good!

The reindeer untangled their reins, WHAT A MESS! and pulled the sleigh to safety, *PHEW!* Santa jumped out with his bag of toys and climbed down the chimney, *HUFF-PUFF.*

Oh, that's good.

No, that's bad!

As he made his way toward the bottom, he got stuck because of his round potbelly, *OOMPH!*

Oh, that's bad.
No, that's good!

The dust in the chimney made Santa sneeze, *AH-CHOO!* and
he was catapulted down to the fireplace, *KA-BOOM!*

Oh, that's good.
No, that's bad!

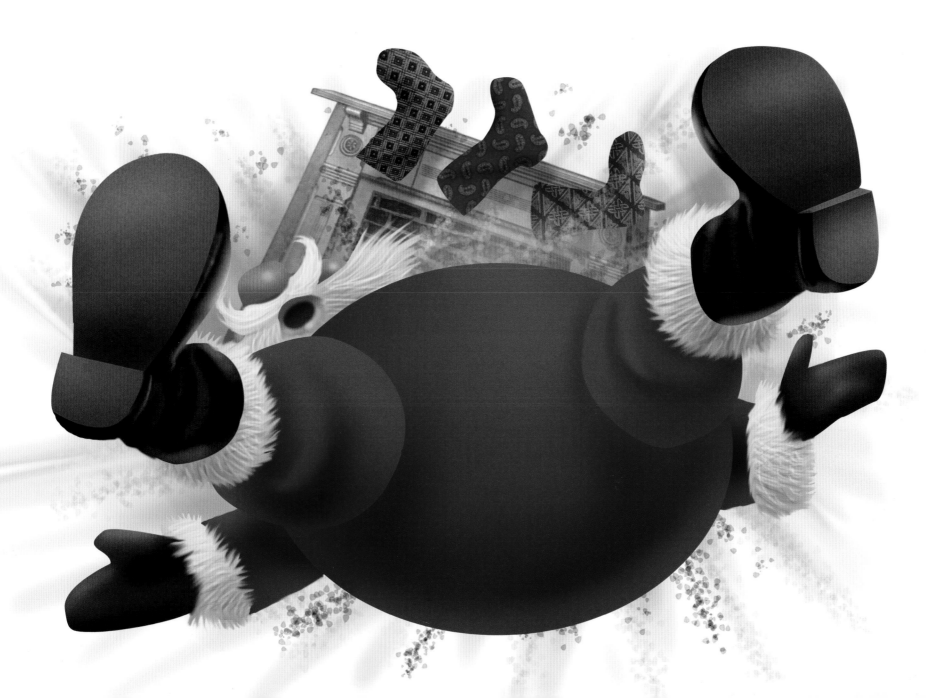

As he crawled into the living room, he tripped over a kitty-cat and bumped his head on a table, *OUCH!* Presents spilled out of his bag, THUMPITY-CLATTER.

Oh, that's bad.
No, that's good!

Santa rubbed his head, patted the kitty, *PUUUURRRRR*, and
picked up all the presents. He stuffed them back into his bag
and stumbled over to the Christmas tree, HOW DAZZLING!

Oh, that's good.
No, that's bad!

As Santa leaned over to put presents under the tree, the
seat of his pants split from top to bottom, *RRRRRIIIIPPPP!*

Oh, that's bad.
No, that's good!

Santa was wearing long underwear beneath his suit, so he tossed his ripped pants into the wastebasket, *SWISH*, held in his stomach, and squeezed back up the chimney, BYE-BYE!

Oh, that's good.
No, that's bad!

When he got to the roof, *PANT-PANT*, he saw that his reindeer had gotten tired of waiting and had flown off without him, OOPS!

Oh, that's bad.
No, that's good!

Santa whistled for his reindeer, TWEET-TWEET,
and they all came flying back, *WHIZZ!*

Oh, that's good.
No, that's bad!

They took off with Santa, *ZOOM-ZOOM,* and as they swerved to avoid a huge pine tree, Santa fell out of the sleigh and landed in a big snowdrift, *PLOPPITY-PLOP!*

Oh, that's bad.
No, that's good!

The reindeer swooped down as Santa struggled out of the snowdrift, OOF!
He jumped back into his sleigh and delivered the rest of the presents,
MERRY CHRISTMAS!

Oh, that's good!
No, that's TERRIFIC!